Clifford
at the Circus

Norman Bridwell

SCHOLASTIC INC.

New York   Toronto   London   Auckland
Sydney   Mexico City   New Delhi   Hong Kong

For Joanne and Thomas Sneed

ISBN 978-0-545-21584-8

Copyright © 1977, 1985 by Norman Bridwell.

All rights reserved. Published by Scholastic Inc.
SCHOLASTIC, CARTWHEEL BOOKS, and associated logos are trademarks and/or registered trademarks of Scholastic Inc.
CLIFFORD, CLIFFORD THE BIG RED DOG, and BE BIG are registered trademarks of Norman Bridwell.

Library of Congress Cataloging-in-Publication Data is available.

20 19 18 17 16   15 16 17

Printed in the U.S.A. 40
This edition first printing, September 2010

I'm Emily Elizabeth,
and I have a dog named Clifford.
We saw a sign that said
the circus was in town.
A smaller sign said the
circus needed help.

We always wanted to join a circus.
We ran there as fast as Clifford could run.

The owner said everything was going wrong.
He didn't think they could put on the show.

I told him Clifford and I would help him.
He didn't think a girl and her dog
could be much help.
But I said, "The show must go on."

The first problem was the lions and tigers.
They wouldn't obey the animal trainer.

Clifford gave them a command.

They listened to Clifford.
After that the animal trainer didn't have to worry anymore.

Some clowns had quit the circus.
The other clowns needed help with their act.
I was sure Clifford could help.

Clifford tried on some costumes.
He found one he liked and joined the act.
Clifford enjoyed being a clown.

He wagged his tail.
That made the act even better.

The tightrope walker had a sprained ankle.
Clifford tried to walk the tightrope.
He was pretty good.

It wasn't his fault that
he couldn't get off the ground.

Before the next act we walked out on the midway.
Clifford loves cotton candy. He sniffed it.

He sniffed a little too hard.

Licking the cotton candy off his nose
made him thirsty. He took a drink.
The circus man tried to stop him.

It was too late.

Clifford had spoiled the high diver's act.

But he didn't spoil the high diver.
Whew, that was close.

The second half of the circus began
with the elephants on parade.
The biggest elephant had a cold in its nose
and couldn't lead the parade.

So Clifford slipped into an elephant suit
and gave them a hand. I mean a tail.

The next act was the human cannon ball.
She didn't have any gunpowder for her cannon.

So Clifford helped her out.

He helped her right out of the tent.

Then came the grand finale.
I was going up in a balloon
with the circus man.
Everyone came out to watch.

Oh dear, the rope broke. I didn't worry.
I knew Clifford would save us.
He rushed to the rescue.

But he missed the rope. We were blowing away.
Things looked bad.

Clifford didn't give up.
He grabbed an extra tent pole.

He used some telephone wire and took aim.

Bull's-eye!

The balloon was falling like a rock.
We were scared silly.

But Clifford got there in time.
Good old Clifford.

Everybody said it was the most exciting end
a circus ever had.
Clifford saved the show, and me.